Walt Disney's

MICKEY MOUSE and GOOFY

The Big Bear Scare

A GOLDEN BOOK, New York
Western Publishing Company, Inc.
Racine, Wisconsin 53404

"It's a beautiful day to go camping!" Mickey Mouse exclaimed as he locked the front door of his house. "Are you sure we have everything?"

"We're all ready to go, Uncle Mickey!" cried Morty. "Ferdie and I packed all the pots and pans and stuff we could possibly need."

"We've been ready to leave since daybreak!" added Ferdie excitedly.

"And *I've* packed enough food in my backpack for three days, Mickey!" Goofy said. "At first, I couldn't get it all in, but I finally found room for everything."

Mickey smiled. "That's great! I'm glad we've all planned so carefully for this trip. The tent's ready to put up as soon as we get to our campsite."

"Uncle Mickey, let's follow the new bike trail out to the lake," Ferdie suggested.

"Okay, boys," Mickey agreed. "That's a good idea."

The hike began well. Sunshine warmed the breeze, and the birds sang happy songs. After a while, the friends stopped to snack on some blackberries that Goofy spotted growing beside the trail.

"I think this will be the best camp-out we've ever had," Mickey told his friends.

As Goofy turned around to agree, he tripped over a log and sprawled on the ground. His bulging backpack came open, and everything in it tumbled out onto the grass.

"Oh, no!" Goofy groaned. "You fellows go on and find a good campsite. I'll repack this stuff and catch up as soon as I can."

"Okay, Goofy. We'll have everything set up for supper when you get there with the food," Mickey said.

"See you later!" the nephews called back from the trail.

While Goofy scrambled to put his pack together again, someone just out of sight watched with quiet interest. A hungry mother bear had come to visit her favorite berry patch. She stood behind a bush, only a few feet away from Goofy. Then, when his back was turned, she snatched the largest package and disappeared into the brush.

A few minutes later, Goofy hurried to catch up with his friends, scratching his head in bewilderment. "This time everything fits into my backpack just right," he mumbled. "I wonder why."

"Hi, Goofy!" Mickey greeted his friend at the campsite. "Why don't you start supper while I finish setting up the tent? I'm almost done."

"We've already unpacked the pots and pans, Goofy. We'll help you!" said Morty and Ferdie eagerly.

"Mountain air really makes you hungry, doesn't it, boys?" said Goofy. "We'll have fish tomorrow, but tonight we'll have the steaks I brought in my pack!"

Thinking how good the steaks would taste, Goofy hurriedly opened his backpack. "Here are the marshmallows — and the bread — and the peanut butter — and the pancake mix. And here —" He stopped suddenly. "The steaks! The steaks are gone!"

"They can't be!" Mickey exclaimed.

"I must have left them at the place where my backpack fell open!" explained Goofy.

"Well," Mickey said, "that's not so bad. We'll just follow the trail back there and get them. Come on! Let's hurry!"

The four campers ran down the trail. When they came to the berry bushes, however, the missing steaks were nowhere to be found.

"I've spoiled the best camping trip ever," Goofy said sadly. "How could I have lost them?" He would not be comforted, no matter what Mickey and the nephews said to him.

Meanwhile, at the camp, three uninvited guests had arrived. The mother bear and her two cubs had come to visit. The cubs quickly discovered that banging pans together was fun. Their mother decided that the tent made a great den, and she settled down comfortably inside it.

"What's that racket?" Mickey wondered as they returned to their camp. Cautiously they hid in the brush nearby and peered into the clearing.

"Oh, no! Bear cubs!" Ferdie moaned.

"Shh!" warned Mickey. "Maybe they'll leave soon. It's funny they haven't eaten those marshmallows yet."

Suddenly Morty realized what must have happened to their steaks. "I'll bet they aren't hungry! *They're* the ones who ate our steaks!"

"Uncle Mickey!" Ferdie whispered. "Look! Something's moving inside our tent!"

"Grrrrr," rumbled the mother bear softly as she turned over to lie on her other side.

"It must be the cubs' mother!" Mickey said worriedly. "How will we ever get her out of there?"

I have to do something, Goofy thought to himself. *Otherwise, our whole trip will be spoiled — and it will be my fault.* He noticed a pail of water standing near the firewood, and it gave him an idea.

While Mickey and the boys watched anxiously, Goofy crawled out of the brush, straight to the pail of water. He had never moved so quietly and carefully in his life. Grasping the pail, he slowly inched his way back into the brush.

Now, Goofy thought as he hid behind a large tree trunk, *I'll climb this tree and dump the water on the bears. A shower should scare them away!*

However, the cubs had seen the pail disappear into the bushes and were watching for it to reappear. Soon they saw the pail moving slowly and jerkily up the side of a tree trunk!

"Here comes the mother bear!" Mickey warned. "She wants to see why the cubs are so quiet."

FIREWOOD
Please don't

Climbing the tree was more difficult than Goofy had imagined. *I must be high enough now,* he thought as he reached for an overhead branch. He peeked around the trunk and prepared to take aim. And what did he see? He saw all three bears — staring right at *him!*

Goofy was so frightened that he lost his hold on both the branch and the pail of water. "HELP!" he cried.

CRASH! SPLASH! Leaves, branches, pail and water, *and* Goofy all plunged down, flattening the tent!

Startled, the mother bear decided that she and her cubs had had enough of this strange place. They ran off, disappearing into the thick woods.

"The bears have left! The bears have left!" all four campers cheered with relief.

Safe beside the campfire that evening, Morty said, "We've had an exciting day!"

"Goofy's pancakes tasted almost as good as steak," Ferdie added contentedly.

"And Goofy found just the right way to send the bears home," praised Mickey. "He saved the whole trip!"

"Aw, it wasn't anything," Goofy said shyly, but he had a grin from ear to ear as he spoke. After all, it isn't everyone who can scare away not one, not two, but *three* bears — all by himself!